Narrative Poetry:

Real-World Wonders and Fictional Delights

By Joyce Jacobo

ISBN: 979-8-9851814-2-5

Dedicated—

To kind souls everywhere

Hope these poems make you smile. ^_^

Table of Contents

Poetry

Acknowledgements

This collection couldn’t have come true without support from my friends (online and off-line) and my family. You know who you are, and you are wonderful. ^_^

Poetry

A Creative Writing Morning

I'm going to have a Creative Writing Morning

right after a hearty breakfast for strength and endurance

to plunge into the depths of Imagination

where anything can emerge

I am going to equip myself accordingly for the task ahead

with a sturdy notebook

plenty of pens

sharpened pencils

and a steaming cup of green tea

just for a bit of an extra treat

accompanied by a sleepy black kitty

who often gurgles and rolls over

for an all-too-important belly scratch

between ideas and considerations

I will open the window to let in a fresh breeze

and listen to the cadences of a light drizzle

pattering along the wooden fence near my window

atop the roof

and upon the grass below

I can be in this world of milky, clouded skies and rainfall

while also venturing forth among landscapes of various climes

that suggest developments even as I shape each segment

of printed text

A Creative Writing Morning...

this happy reality spent in the creation of fantasies

and dreams come true

[1]Archway of Hope

It appears at the edge of many storms

even the darkest (or perhaps especially so)

when breaks appear

in the clouds that loom overhead

to let in the light

while a light drizzle

might still fall like gentle

caresses upon

those below

An archway of color

constructed in mid-air

that slopes upward

and then downward

a light ribbon

offered as a consolation

[1] Inspired by an event where, as a graduate student meeting up with my classmates in a conference room after a tiring day, we peered out a window and noticed a rainbow arching down into the parking lot. It appeared to be less than a mile from where we were and was quite vibrant.

for those who

keep their chins up despite the weariness

stormy weather can bring

Such a hopeful sight is a much finer treasure

than any pot

(or maybe pots)

of gold

one might find at either end—

a natural miracle for all to share

and therefore invaluable

Old Face

Last night I helped to repair an old clock

that had stood still on our piano for too many years

protected by a glass dome

A cleaning with a simple rag

revealed a grand old face with hands

like twirled ribbons frozen

at half past 2:00

and the words "Rhythm Quartz"

as a signature poised in the middle

This clock used to rest among so many glass figurines and pieces

in a room with silk curtains that fluttered in the slightest breeze

like pleasant ghosts who waved hello to visitors

with a much larger twin that at every hour

sang out like Big Ben

to fill that entire house with music

...often accompanied by the hums

of a gentle older voice

That image has been frozen in time in my mind

ever since childhood

like a photograph mislaid and forgotten

at the bottom of a box

or an old clock

in plain sight for so long

gazes can past by

without comment

Is it strange

that all it took was two batteries placed

in the right spaces

to make the gold-plated bells swing back and forth again

or to allow the three pairs of dancers in their little ballroom

to twirl around a central column

with great animation

or to bring back long-neglected memories

that offer so much comfort

amid these difficult times?

Is it also peculiar to note

that while the old clock on the piano

will never sing like its larger twin

every time I pass the piano

I cannot help but remember

those bells

mixed by hums

in accompaniment

...and glimpse

an old face?

Dinosaur Eggs[2]

While living out in Michigan for a year

in the little town of West Olive

our mother would often take

my brother and I

on a prehistoric quest

"Let's find dinosaur eggs!"

she proclaimed before helping us

to tug on sturdy shoes and hats—

and then we would venture into the forest

that surrounded our maternal grandparents' home

Birds tweeted high in the ancient trees

squirrels skittered among the brush

and deer considered us around trunks

as dragonflies whizzed through the air—

[2] As far as I understand it, this specific area in Michigan has since been turned into Hemlock Park. A wonderful place preserved for everyone to appreciate nature.

just as they had for centuries

We never found so much as dinosaur tracks

but we did take strolls along streams

enjoyed detours to the homes of other relatives

and took shelter beneath fragrant pine trees

when caught amid light rainstorms

Then we would come home

and our mother would boil eggs

freshly gathered from the local market—

fondly remembered

many years later

Virtual Tour in 2020[3]

Today…

I visited the Smithsonian Museum of Natural History

for the first time

where countless treasures—

all tributes to various time periods

waited around every corner

An elephant upon a raised pedestal greeted me

in the front lobby

from which numerous corridors extended

that led to rooms dominated

by ancient undersea marvels

mysterious fossils

dinosaur skeletons

gemstone collections

and even a butterfly garden

I read information on prehistoric times

[3] Based on a digital version of their Museum of Natural History that the Smithsonian made available starting in 2020.

toured the café area

then jumped at the sight

of an enormous shark

which filled

my computer screen

. . . so many wonders

to lift the spirits and

broaden the mind

given as digitized gifts

from the guardians

of those treasures

just for us

Dove in a Hurricane[4]

Several years ago   if memory still serves me well

a massive hurricane devastated several towns

deep in the Midwest

Houses got torn apart amid the wildness of nature

but families paid the greatest toll

and the lives they had built

Emergency crews rushed to help those in need

to rescue the survivors from the debris

and comfort them

despite the fractured stability

scattered across the land

As they shifted through the wreckage

of an old barn

an odd melody echoed into the stillness

that gave them pause—

the unmistakable coo

[4] True story. That dove was an inspiration.

of a dove

from somewhere beneath

the torn wooden beams

muffled yet strong

The crews dug through the ruins

and came upon

a miraculous pocket of space in which a dove

dirty

with both wings broken

had sung despite the darkness and pain

for what they estimated

must have been at least two days

Later members of the crew would theorize to news reporters

the songs had kept the dove alive with hope

called out into the world

because even a tragedy could never

take them away

Furry Bodies at Play

I opened the door one early morning

a mug of chamomile tea in hand

to find two furry visitors at play

around the decrepit couch that stands

upon my wooden front porch

Two weasels at graceful ease with life

hopped about each other

on a discarded blanket

that had a flower pattern

as if among a vast field

Their coats were mostly the hue

of moistened soil

that lightened to tints long the bellies

like brown sugar

with dark little masks on the face

where a dollop of white

much like whipped cream

on a miniature pastry

While one would scale one side

of the couch to the top

to race along

toward the other end

then to glance around before the descent

the other would tug

at the blanket with tiny teeth

shoot behind the folds

and out again

only to await until the partner

returned to the bottom

before the next shot up the couch

Always in motion for minutes on end

they paused only once to realize

I was at the door

then went on with the game

for a while longer

before they streaked away into a bush

Not as if frightened away

by their audience

but simply done

until another day of play

Parade on the Water

I used to believe parades

always flowed along pathways

composed of solid ground

from dirt to hard stone

with floats that bobbed

over their audiences

as giant balloons

or massive floats

on wheels

But two evenings ago

I got introduced to a Parade of Lights—

where boats that came in various shapes

and sizes coasted along a circular route

within a harbor fringed by the spectators

Each vessel came lit up with their own display

from

strings

of

bright

lights

TO GIANT INFLATABLE SANTAS AND SNOW PEOPLE

which shone into the darkness

and gleamed upon the water

attended every once in a while

by the proclamations of curious seals

who splashed about the procession

Holiday tunes echoed through the air

from old carols to Grinchy delights

while the shadowy sailors

cried out their best wishes

for a wondrous Christmas season

I sat upon rocks

surrounded by my friend and her family

and friends of that family

with whom I made friends as well

on that enchanted night

where the way I saw parades changed

and I felt a New Year approach

with nothing other than excitement

Rainbow Patch

After a long and fretful night

where even dreams were afraid to come

dawn pours past the curtains

at just the right angle through the window

to create a rectangle of bright colors

upon the wall opposite my bed

like a single patch in a much larger quilt

created on a natural prism

offered to chase away the shadows

that lingered

. . . a good omen

for a week defined

by concerns

. . . or a random coincidence

unexpected but pleasant

. . . or perhaps

(and even better)

Both

Spirited Halloween Echoes[5]

It seeks out emptied buildings

in which the echoes of businesses

often long-standing but now departed

still remain

Like a lonely firefly

searching for kindred spirits

whom once found

get stoked full of vigor

as they participate in a tribute

to all things altered over time

or that await

hidden in the shadows

Mortal visitors come

to marvel at decorations

wide-ranging as spiderwebs

[5] Inspired by the Spirit of Halloween stories that often appear in empty store spaces around Halloween each year. Every time I step into one of them, especially ones once occupied by businesses I've visited in the past, I become aware how just how many memories such a place can hold even after the inventory within it has changed drastically.

bubbling cauldrons

and rubbery bats

activate animatronics

frightful as howling wolves

cackling clowns

and jumping spiders

or discover adornments

appealing as skeleton bones

masquerade masks

and vampire capes

Past laughter

mixes with present delights—

all to serve fleeting guests

between one season

and the next

until the spooky festivities

allow the remnants of all the memories

formed within those walls

to slip away

alongside the Harvest Moon

...to make way for another year

of fresh starts

until October

once again

approaches

Written Candle Wishes

I heard of a woman who every Christmas

lit candles to give her wishes

to those around the world

in need of extra comfort

People she knew and would never know

for her family members to find true happiness

or for lost children to reach their homes safely

or for the terminally ill to improve in health

That kindly soul could fill her whole backyard

with all the wishes she wanted to give

they got sent out through candleflames

which flickered in the winter darkness

But this year she cannot light those many candles

so I choose to light them in my own way

through the only method I able to offer

in the form of a very simple poem

It is a candle formed by words across a page

with a bright flame ignited by anyone
able to read the hopes that are here
for everyone throughout the world

As the charitable woman would always do
I give my best wishes to those in need
for the sick in mind or body to get well
and that compassion will hold them close

I also wish the candlelight set out in this very spot
will encourage other people to make candles
lit by words that relate their best wishes
during the holiday season and into the future

Secret Santa

I heard a family struggled one Christmas season

in the wintry heart of the Great Depression

even to place enough food on the table

much less manage a big celebration

They numbered five in total

two young girls and one even younger boy

attended by parents much too careworn

after the father had lost his employment

However despite the little they had

the family often lent a hand to their neighbors

in countless ways

from kind words exchanged to errands run

They were simple acts of kindness that

within a huge city

might just get overlooked—

except they mattered a great deal

for those to whom they came so rarely

Then on the night of Christmas Eve

when the three children talked of magical deliveries

while the parents stifled their tears at the lack of jollity

they foresaw for the next morning

there came a knock upon the front door

followed by a bellow of cheery laughter

which belonged as the door opened

to Santa Claus himself

The jolly old elf entered the home

with a large bag of toys

accompanied by (to the parent's surprise)

oddly familiar elves

each with bags filled with food

As all looked on in wonder

the visitors unpacked their offerings

Santa Claus had gifts for the children

while the elves laid out a feast

at the table

They even brought in a fir tree

that Santa Claus and his crew

helped to decorate

And then Santa and his assistants slipped away

just before midnight struck

as if they feared a spell might end

The person who told me this tale said

no one ever claimed credit for that glorious delivery

so it could have only been Santa Claus

for he comes in various shapes

carried along from one house to the next

in the hearts of those who show others they care...

So I believe Santa Claus came that night

I believe it with all my heart.

Night Music

Once when evening filled the countryside

I felt inspired to pull out my harmonica

(a simple tremolo)

and serenade the full silver moon

with an idle melody

that never received a name

Seated beside an opened bedroom window

the gentle cadence flowed out

into the crisp darkness like a lullaby

Until I became aware of an extra note

amid the proceedings

regular and distinct

I paused long enough to peer into the dimness

where soon concentration

combined with pale moonlight

revealed the form of a barn owl

seated upon the chain-link fence

that surrounded the yard

A lone barn owl who

fell silent for several held breaths as I stared

before another soft croon vibrated into the night

as if in hesitation

With something like fascinated wonder

I played a few notes on my harmonica

then paused

at which point the barn owl

with head cocked to one side

called into the night

in response

This odd exchange went on

for more than a minute

Before with a sudden flap of wings

the barn owl came to rest on the earth

beyond my bedroom window

We studied each other at close range

Eyes that reflected the radiant moon
gave me an even stare
while I gazed back in astonishment
It was like an enchantment
or perhaps a fairytale made real
until the owl flew off in a flurry of wings
toward the distant mountains
overhung by stars
I would later wonder
if the owl got frightened away
with the realization I was human
or if my unexpected accompaniment
knew what I was the whole time
and wanted to know how it felt
to share a song with one of us
Stranger things have happened
but I will always remember that owl
and when we made music together

A Spirited Museum[6]

There exists an enchanted wonderland
deep within the city of Mitaka in Japan
reached by the crossing of a boundary
between city and forest
to glimpse a massive building
decorated in the bright colors
of illustrated creativity

A huge plush creature
with an enormous belly and wide grin
awaits in the ticket office out front
known as Totoro
while high atop the roof
an ancient humanoid robot stands guard
even while vines cling to its long arms
and wrap about its broad-shouldered frame

[6] Based on the Studio Ghibli Museum that celebrates, well, Studio Ghibli. It would be lovely to visit this wonderful place in person someday.

I have only heard of all its wonders

dreamed up by a legendary animation studio

whose creations reside there in various forms

...such as frescoes where witches fly on broomsticks

pigs pilot red airplanes

and fish turn into young girls

...or a room where children play inside and around

a large cat shaped like a bus

(or perhaps a bus shaped like a cat)

...or the miniature Saturn theater

where short films play for audiences

every day

One floor to the next

constructed from designs by an animator who

yearned for a place where visitors could walk away

more at peace with themselves and the world

than before they came

...almost like therapy through artistry

Court of Cats

Have you ever known the legend
related to those fog-filled woods
near a certain town in the Southwest
where on every full-moon evening
small and clever community members
gather within a secretive glen—
known only as "The Court of Cats?"
An ancient spirit shaped as a massive oak tree
presides over the proceedings
while its thick roots create convenient rows
upon which all the feline attendants sit
and listen as a silent jury to each case
Only a single human knows of these strange events
an old woman once a lawyer in a huge city
(or so the townspeople say)
still sharp of mind and sound of judgement who
on certain evenings receives a telephone call

(for the ways of cats and magic are strange)

as an invitation to use her skills once more

deep in the forest

. . . which she keeps in strict confidentiality

What might happen there and why

I (as the writer) can only begin to fathom

but those same townspeople have also said

the local cats are always quite content

and knowing in their ways

so perhaps that

is a good clue

of this harmonious system

The Lantern Girl

A young fisherman was lost at sea

somewhere off the coast of Japan

amid the darkest evening he had known

After a sudden storm

that had pushed him an unknown distance

he struggled just to stay afloat

while enshrouded by dense fog

The fisherman cried out for help

in his desperation

as he bobbed atop the choppy waves

and rain drummed down from the heavens

hidden from sight

He just avoided a sharp slither of stone

which jabbed up from the ocean

much like a curved sword

then another that scraped the hull

from the other side

The fisherman realized

he was in a minefield

of these vicious obstacles

and despaired at his chances

to escape them to safety

when there came

a glimmer of red light

shaped into a radiant sphere

It glided through the air like a firefly

and produced soft music

that reminded him of a lullaby

The fisherman followed the light

with great care in his boat

past the jagged stones

until his boat stopped

in a harsh jerk

against soft sand

and the fog cleared to reveal

he had reached a village

along the coast

***

The storm had blown him

to a place many miles away

from his usual grounds

By the miracle of the red light

the fisherman learned

he had navigated a vast stretch

of the sharp stones in the fog

that had claimed many lives

over the years

He asked after this odd occurrence

throughout the village

until he came across an old man

who tended a shrine upon a hill

that overlooked the sea

This old man told of a girl

who lost her father

(a sailor)

to the stones

and would forever afterwards

help to guide ships away

from the stones from atop that hill

whenever the fog rolled in

with a red paper lantern

Although it was amid the sea

rather than from the hill

that the fisherman had seen the light

he refused to question the fact but asked

to meet with this lantern girl and thank her

To which the old man gestured to the shrine

and indicated the girl had grown old

then passed away

only the previous week

Shifted Story Gears

Once scientists threw what they perceived

as a bunch of rusty metal and junk

right beside a sign on the outskirts to their city

that read, "Welcome to Smudge—

Home to the legendary Steampunk Lab"

with a note attached underneath,

"Under New Management."

Once a young mechanic on her evening journey home

(after the completion of a grueling project)

found an old robot scattered into limbs and parts

abandoned beside a welcome sign among an assortment

of shattered bottles

empty food wrappers

soda cans

broken appliances

deflated tires

and unmarked

steel barrels.

Once a dream played out in the memory of a lab assistant

built by a scientist with a kind face and dimpled cheeks who

grew older and older more wizened and hunched

while other scientists whose faces were serene in her presence

(but severe in her absence)

increased

until... the day...

her creator was...

gone.

Once a robot woke up on the wooden worktable

in the loft space of a tumbledown barn—

that belonged to a tired but enthusiastic mechanic

(dressed in overalls and sturdy work boots)

who encouraged him to wiggle his tube-like arms

flex his rubber glove hands

dig through his toolbox contents

(contained within his spacious box-shaped body)

and swivel his globe-shaped head

...then apologized for his continued lack of legs

(which she made up for with new straps

that would allow the mechanic to carry him around

like a backpack).

Once a mechanic named Myra Crankshaft introduced herself

to a robotic lab assistant called Gearbox

and proposed a new life on the road for them both

as mechanics-for-hire and freelancers

who roamed from one location to the next

to fix machinery long neglected

in distant locations

and help the people there.

Once two companions left a decrepit barn

to cut their own path across a barren plain

away from a vast city

where the steam and smoke from factories filled the skies

and the noises of massive pumps and assembly lines

echoed in a regular rhythm throughout the day and night—

while a spiraling tower topped by a purplish globe

loomed at its center.

Once two travelers went forth

into a world the mechanic had only heard tales about

from people the robot had never known

...together

to discover new stories

they would make

for themselves.

Mystic Desert[7]

I know a desert land where spectral stagecoaches

rumble through the night

never to reach ladies dressed in wedding gowns

who forever pace well-worn stations

desperate to reunite with distant lovers

White horses once owned by bandits

now run wild and free among hills

in which ill-gained bounties

have been hidden for more than a century

Small flames flit around certain mountains

while skeletons with lanterns in their ribcages wander

in constant search for treasure-leaden mines lost to time

Coyotes yowl beneath the full moon inhabited by a kind goddess

[7] Inspired by my hometown.

and in the summer greedy spirits dance

about an old well in happiness

at riches they cannot touch

Owls guide gentle souls to their eternal slumber

safe from a malicious being

known for thunderstorms and meteors

exiled to a mountain peak by the ancestors of a people

whose descendants still inhabit the land

To passersby in the day it is a sleepy place

quiet and remote

But to those who know

even a few of its many stories

the desert reveals its magic

and grows in strength

much like the Santa Ana Winds

A Voyage Across the Clouds

Someday we will take a voyage across the clouds—

you and I—

away from all the weighty turbulences

that keep us anchored

in separate harbors

Together we will set sail

towards distant horizons

defined by ethereal dreams to carry our vessel

and the cosmos that stretches overhead

In this liminal space

we can make a home upon those waves

danced on decks stocked with memories

watch our sails flutter like butterfly wings

then breathe in pure jubilation

at what we have created

Until then . . .

. . . let us share these visions

and plan our course

Perhaps we may never captain ships

atop actual clouds

but what we might gain instead

could be just as ideal

or even

grander

truths

A Kitty Wake-Up Call

Sweet kitty cat I can hardly believe

you just reached out

with one little black paw

and

booped me on the nose

I have awoken so many times

to the gentle rumbles of your internal engine

as you lay curled atop the comforter

only inches away from my face

I have awoken some mornings

to the soft spring of your strong legs

up

onto the bed

and felt their pressure

when you balanced atop my arm

until I got up

I have even awoken on occasion

to hear the commotion of a plush bird

attached by a string

to the tip of a stick

as you dragged it down the hall

through the ajar door

right to my bedside

then meowed aloud

But I have never awoken

to a paw boop upon the nose

at 6:00 in the morning...

...it makes me excited to discover

what antics you will try

tomorrow

...my sweet kitty

alarm clock

Straight and Simple Path

I have sometimes heard of but never found

a simple unchanged path

through life

like a velvet carpet unfurled

straight to grand goals

such as Success

or Wisdom

or Inner peace—

So far most of the paths I have ever known

stretch for an interminable distance

and swirl about

in unpredictable ways

more akin

to a ribbon tousled

by a breeze

They might extend

right into dense thickets that scratch

at exposed ankles

lead amid wild groves

where unnamed dangers prowl

and loop back on themselves

to intersect with other paths

until it is impossible to tell

where I have left one

then started on another

...among many

similar difficulties

Even so along those intertangled ways

towards countless destinations

I have stumbled across beautiful flowers

around sudden bends

seen bright rainbows

after heavy rainstorms

made friends of fellow travelers who

shared the same (or different) places

they hoped to reach

gazed upon odd locations

born in the mystical realm of reality

beyond what I could have imagined

and reflected on existential questions

which developed

amid long stretches of silence

Each turn of the road

has granted a new memory

often with a lesson to match

like personalized souvenirs

...unquantified but substantial enough

to fill up

my mind and soul

....and maybe

it is in the twists experienced

while on the road

that we find

our true destinations

Birthright

Every moment is a meteoric streak

bright and fleeting

across the formidable expanse

of time

and space

Moments given to us by the universe

to grasp like golden threads

that drift down from the heavens—

the perfect material

for woven futures

of our own designs

Opportunities to stand on hilltops that overlook

vast pastures and crystalline lakes

run along trails through forests

where sunshine pours down like waterfalls

from the canopy overhead

and to even feel small

from the deck of a ship

far out at sea

away from any land

Excitement and thrills

unique for each person who experiences them—

to share with family members

friends

and generations to come

All these things are our blessings

from the first second

we came to exist and grow

as stardust beings

in a grand universe

of wonders

...never to take

for granted

Chloe Violin[8]

It feels as if I've

brought home a peculiar creature

with a delicate light body

that lays along one of my arms

as I stroke its belly

in attempts to stir melodies

Most of those caresses so far

have resulted in scratchy and uneasy notes—

and the snapping of a string or two

which needed replacement

Each mistake (however)

is a learning experience

where I have begun to realize

the subtle complexity of its aspects

alongside the ways they flow

[8] Inspired by getting a violin. ^_^

into a unified whole

On occasion I even find

a sweet sonorous tone

slips into my bow strokes

like signs of acceptance

from my new wooden companion

that someday

we might very well

make beautiful music

together

Fairy Tale Route

Someday I would love to venture

along that mystical pathway

known as "Fairy Tale Route"—

which weaves among foothills and forests

deep

in

Germany

to trace the lives

of the Brothers Grimm

from their birthplace in Hanau

off to locations where they preserved

fairytales like literary butterflies given

havens within the pages of books

such as Alsfeld

...where "Red Riding Hood" first

risked the woods for her grandmother

or Bad Wildungen

...that saw “Snow White” grace their streets

with her lordly father who controlled the mines

to Reinhardswald

...near which “Sleeping Beauty” once slept

in Sababurg Castle

and Hamelin

...famed for the desertion

of rats and children

lured away by music

all the way to Bremen

... that animal musicians sought to reach

and their statues

at last succeeded

A road traveled

over the course of centuries

then alluded to in beloved stories—

there to offer a journey

between fantasy and reality

...like a dream

from once

upon

a time

Literary Structures

A simple pen touched to a blank canvas page

can lay the foundation for a new chapter

in many textual lives—

born from words to breathe

upon each reading

Stories flow like thoughts

uninterrupted

separate from the actual process

of actual starts

and stops

Leading guest readers deep

along pathways crafted

especially for them

Amid a universe bound

together by a single spine

Impressions formed

as gifts for generations to come

with characters and unique experiences

for visitors to wander about

as through structures

refurbished through reprintings

or perhaps simply retellings

A Moment of Happy Misidentification

At an odd little moment

within a store like so many others...

Two families cross paths—

an elderly couple

and a mother with her young child

"Grandpa!" the child waves a mittened hand

her face brightened

by a broad smile

The elderly man—

so distracted and careworn until then—

smiles in surprise   and then keeps on smiling

Laughter gets exchanged

before the families take their own paths

each one a bit happier

than they were before

Idle Daydreaming

Do you ever set aside daily routines
to let your mind wander around
in unrestricted directions
like a child released
upon a playground?

Just for a few moments
where ideas can flutter about
and intermingle
but then get blown away
by reality
as dandelion seeds might
by a stray breeze

Those trips can become extra valves to twist
to release stress-filled steam
while the imagination wanders
in-between one activity
and the next

Sometimes I get so busy

that I forget to let loose

until

caught in a sudden

quiet period

I slip deep into inner distractions

from which I often surface

with a gasp

of relief

...thanks to a pause

for dreams to take hold

in the daylight

A Sketch in Estrangement[9]

A tall rectangular object

stands made from wood

with a bronze knob

positioned to the right

side of its viewed surface

Turn the knob

and pull

to reveal a reality

different than the one

in which you reside

Step

into

that

reality

Find an identical knob

(on the other side)

[9] Estrangement involves seeking to make the familiar something unfamiliar.

push it until a click rings out

and hides where you have been

On some of these portals

you can twist another knob

that locks them against entry

by others

or unlocks them to allow

for easy access

Found in many structures

throughout a much broader world—

all made by hand

or machine

to move

between

one state

(and)

the next

Autumn Delights

Spices waft through the crisp air

like promises of change—

cinnamon

pumpkin

ginger

while tree leaves shift their fashions

to maple syrup hues

right before they

drop down

and perform rustling melodies

in bunches

across the ground

To further the transformation

corn mazes grow tall

pumpkins show off carved grimaces

and people assume disguises

for spooky magical occasions

But what I love   best of all

are the fantastic stories spun by expert weavers—

such as those found around great bonfires

where people dance and apple cider flows as freely

as accounts of phantoms

monsters

and other mysterious forces

Memories from the past

intermingle with legends from centuries ago

which together pass between generations

. . . much like the ending of one chapter in life

and the beginning of the next

Emboldened Words

You are powerful

I want to tug these words off the page
like threads from a much broader quilt
and twist them into a bracelet to place
right around your wrist—
to touch them late at night
when doubts crouch about your bed
and whisper of scars
from years ago
alongside concerns
for tomorrow

You are smart

I yearn to tie this message onto you
in a similar way to a long
and sturdy ribbon
used to hold up your hair—
so you can remember it

at every step taken

until its meaning

becomes

an understood part

...of you

You are loved

I hope to arrange each letter of that truth

as if they were beads along a length of yarn

tied loosely about your neck—

there to lay upon your chest

and harmonize with your heartbeats

like a symphony played

for all the world to hear

at long last

...without hesitation

A Stroll Beneath the Heavens

To help a worn mind and depressed spirit
perhaps tonight I will stroll beneath the heavens
with the Milky Way trail as my path
Among meadows of dry grass cleansed by moonlight
I will wade as if through an oceanic tide
and play melodies upon a harmonica
learned from the Santa Ana Wind
I will listen while coyotes perched on hilltops serenade all creation
then gaze upwards to glimpse crystal butterflies
shimmer on their journey to become distant stars
and wish them good fortune
A raven will land on my shoulder with a pen clasped in his mouth
while an arctic fox will frolic around a small green dragon
and a robed gargoyle will ride a large wolf
Every step I take will sound out a steady heartbeat rhythm
as I try to make sense of the world again
I will follow this cosmic path for however long it takes

over jagged mountains so tall they seem insurmountable

across murky rapids where demons bubble beneath the surface

and through more than a few tangled forests and stone ruins

helped along by my companions

(some made during the journey)—

until we discover enough harmony and warmth

to soothe an aggrieved soul

and create a smile

so we can bring those secrets

all the way back home

. . .to you

A Lost Sole

I remember. ..

I went to the beach

When the tide was high and

the reefs tugged at my sandals

The sand squeezed

between my toes

In calm invitation

We chose to play

A fond and simple game

Of everlasting memory

Ten years have passed

Since I gave my sole

To that distant place

I hope it remembers me.

ABOUT THE AUTHOR

Joyce Jacobo is a freelance writer from SoCal with an MA in Literature & Writing Studies. She is the author of *Literary Observations*, and her shorter works have also appeared in publications such as the *San Diego Poetry Annual*, *Scribes*MICRO*Fiction*, *Planetside*, and *Creative Gems*. She maintains *The Literary Serenity Archives*, a WordPress blog, and is a book reviewer for The US Review of Books.

Printed in Great Britain
by Amazon

23543043R00056